Charo Pita is a writer, storyteller, narrator, singer, mother, and cyclist. She studied Hispanic philology at the University of Salamanca and interpretation at the Santart Theater School. Her inspiration for *Thank You!* came while she was taking a walk during the winter solstice. She lives in Spain.

Anuska Allepuz grew up in Spain, where she studied fine arts at the University of Salamanca. She went on to receive a master's degree in children's book illustration at the Cambridge School of Art. Her previous books include *That Fruit Is Mine!* (Albert Whitman) and *The Boy, the Bird, and the Coffin Maker* (Philomel). She lives in South London.

Thank you for so many great travel companions.
Thank you for your silences and your
words—for your company.

— C. P.

Thank you to my family! My mother, Alex,
Alberto, Mariona, and Jana.

— A. A.

FSC
www.fsc.org
MIX
Paper from
responsible sources
FSC® C104723

First published in the United States in 2019
by Eerdmans Books for Young Readers
an imprint of Wm. B. Eerdmans Publishing Co.,
Grand Rapids, Michigan
www.eerdmans.com/youngreaders

Originally published in Spain under the title *¡Gracias!*
© 2013 Ediciones la fragatina
English-language translation © 2019 Pip Manley

Manufactured in China

27 26 25 24 23 22 21 20 19   1 2 3 4 5 6 7 8 9

Library of Congress Cataloging-in-Publication Data

Names: Pita, Charo, author. | Allepuz, Anuska, 1979- illustrator.
Title: Thank you! / written by Charo Pita ; illustrated by Anuska Allepuz.
Other titles: ¡Gracias! English
Description: Grand Rapids MI : Eerdmans Books for Young Readers, 2019. |
    Summary: Isabella is full of questions about her world, and while Grandma
    cannot answer them, she does know what to do when faced with a mystery.
Identifiers: LCCN 2019004354 | ISBN 9780802855244
Subjects: | CYAC: Grandmothers—Fiction. | Questions and answers—Fiction. |
    Gratitude—Fiction. | Nature—Fiction.
Classification: LCC PZ7.P64267 Th 2019 | DDC [E]—dc23 LC record available at
https://lccn.loc.gov/2019004354

Thank You!

Written by
Charo Pita

Illustrated by
Anuska Allepuz

Eerdmans Books for Young Readers

Grand Rapids, Michigan

It was getting late. Isabella and her grandma were chatting about the world.

"Grandma," said Isabella, "you know everything. Tell me, why does the sea stop at the sand, instead of swallowing up the whole town with its watery mouth?"

Grandma didn't say anything. Isabella listened to her silence for a while.

The water sang in the quietness.

"Grandma!" exclaimed the little girl.
"You know everything. Tell me, what holds
the moon up so it doesn't fall out of the sky?"

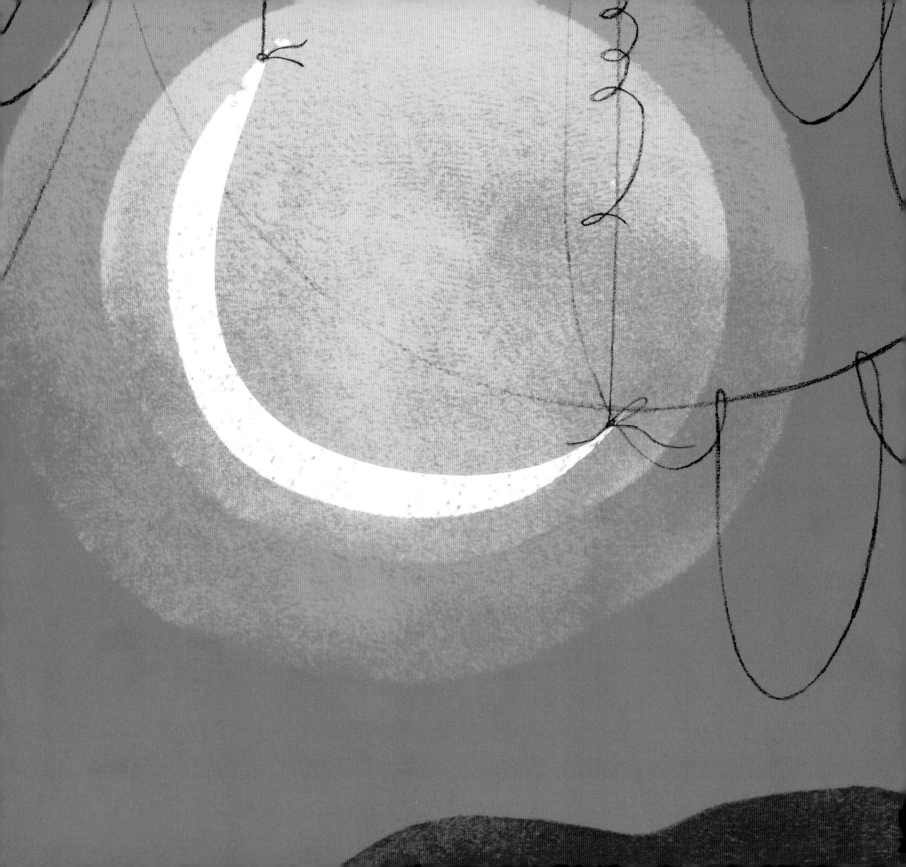

"Who paints the clouds, Grandma? What makes the wind blow?"
Grandma opened her mouth, as if she were about to say something.

Isabella held her breath . . .

At last, she would know everything!

But Grandma only gave a small sigh.

Isabella refused to give up.
"Now that winter is coming," she asked,
"why don't the days get shorter and
shorter, until they disappear altogether?
Who turns on the sun's light?
Grandma! GRANDMA! Why aren't
you saying anything?"

"Because I don't know the answers," said Grandma.

"You don't?"

"No. But I do know what we have to do with all of these mysteries."

Grandma gestured to Isabella. The two of them went down to the beach, took off their shoes, and walked to the water's edge. A wave broke on the sand, washing over their feet, and then went back out again.

"Thank you, sea!" said Grandma.

"Thank you!" said Isabella.

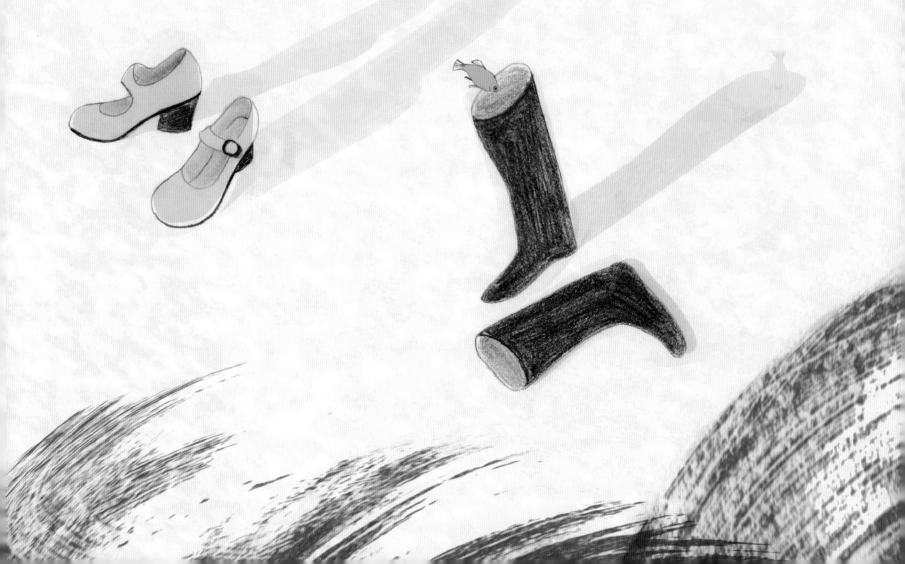

Little by little, the daylight began to fade.
The moon was already outlined in the sky.

Then Grandma smiled at the moon and
exclaimed, "Thank you, moon! Thank you!"

"Thank you! Thank you!" the little girl
exclaimed with a smile.

They played a game of looking for shapes in the clouds.
They threw a piece of colored string into the wind
to decorate its tail.

"Thank you, wind! Thank you, clouds! Thank you!"
they shouted at the same time.

Grandmother and granddaughter walked westward toward town. The sun disappeared completely, and the day turned to night.

"Come back! We'll be waiting for you!" they called to the sun, waving goodbye to it.

"And . . . THAAAAANK YOOOU!"

Then they went back home.
They had dinner and brushed their teeth.

Just like every other night, Isabella got into bed
and sat watching as Grandma told a story.

"Grandma," Isabella said suddenly, "why has time
drawn pictures on your face?"

"I don't know, Isabella,"
Grandma replied.

Faced with this new mystery, the two of them sat in silence.

Then Isabella took Grandma's hand, with wrinkles drawn all over it, and whispered in her ear: "Thank you, Grandma!"